From Black Bottom to Liberation

Surviving the streets of Detroit

OMARI KHALFANI

WOODSON D. ALLEN JR
A.K.A. BEANNIE

ISBN:0692325263
ISBN-13:978-0692325261

ACKNOWLEDGEMENT

For this writing, I would like to take a moment to recognize and say "Thanks" to some people who have been instrumental in my life as a writer and as a person. This thank you begins with God the Father, His son Jesus and the Holy Spirit.

Thanks to my lovely wife of eighteen years, Jackie, who had faith in my writing and who has worked long hours to assist me in bringing this book to life, also much appreciation goes to my two sons Woodson David Allen, III ("Scooter") and Lamar J. Allen. Appreciation also goes to my best friends in Detroit, Tim, Ricky, and Tiwanna ("Pee Wee"). I would like to thank many other friends, and my many supportive family members including my St. Clair family who all helped me in so many wonderful ways. Much love to Mr. Brown of Brown's Barber

College who was my teacher and mentor. Additionally, I must thank my grandmother Aura Sangster, her sister my dear Aunt Nelly for being so instrumental and such great influences in my life. And finally, so much appreciation goes to my church family at Light of the World Christian Tabernacle in Stockbridge, Georgia. Bishop Ruth Holmes, who I also call mom, is also a mentor and inspiration to all.

CONTENTS

INTRODUCTION

I grew up in the rough and dangerous streets of Detroit, Michigan. I made it through a dysfunctional household despite being degraded by the person I loved the most, my mother, and abandoned by my father for many years.

I was drawn to the wrong people and did many things such as roaming the streets late at night with no supervision, drinking, cursing, partying, fighting, carrying weapons, having sex, and using drugs, by the age of twelve, which are things that simply should not have been a part of a young child's life.

I was constantly told I would end up in jail or dead and that I would never amount to anything. It seems everything was considered except the things that would change it all God, prayer, and church. It was not in a moment and took a long time, but I survived it all through prayer from many good family members, good friends, using my will and determination, and receiving help from people who were not even related to me. I can now tell my story through this book and let others know they can make it also.

Many names have been changed to protect the innocent but the stories are all true as I recall my life back then and now.

I am a barber now by trade, I have two great children, and a beautiful wife, all whom I love dearly. I know that certain people and things are placed in our paths for various reasons but divine power is there also and if we tap into it we can be changed. We need to listen and answer our calling.

I didn't always listen to the positive people in my life and mostly took the wrong paths early on, but deep inside I knew I could be better than I was. There were times when I felt fearful and I didn't feel strong. Some of these feelings still rise up, but I just keep pushing onward knowing that I can be better. I have learned to persevere, do what is right, keep my head up, and my feet firmly planted on the ground. I hope that you will enjoy reading this book and that it will encourage you to do the same.

Omari Khalfani

.

1
BLACK BOTTOM

As far back as I can remember I started

out in a place called the Black Bottom in Detroit,

Michigan. Life started out innocent for me, but I

did not know that I would go through hell. My

mother, father and three other siblings lived in

our house. My mom had three other children

before I came along. My grandfather lived across

the street. I couldn't have been much more than

four at the time; I remember the house having

rats, roaches, and a black and white television

set that we had to put a clothes hanger on to make it work because there was no antenna. Strangely enough it still felt like home. I watched my mother and my grandfather's second wife, Odessa, wash clothes in this big old round thing that had a ringer which squeezed the clothes through. They called it a wash tub. After the clothes squeezed through they would hang them outside to dry on the clotheslines or if it was cold or raining they would hang them over this big black pot belly stove we had.

Even at that young age, I was restless. I would roam the alleys looking at the dogs, chickens, roosters and hens in other people's backyards. Sometimes I would get a big jar of water, go outside and skeet water at people – especially our neighbors. That was fun! My momma used to take us kids over to our "Big Momma" our grandmother's apartment a lot. Her apartment had an elevator man who would take us up and down. We loved playing in the halls and on the elevators. We would run up and down the hall playing tag until one of us would get mad when we got tagged and then we declared that we would never play it again. But we always did, whenever we got the chance.

2
STOEPLE STREET

We moved to Stoeple Street when I turned five. It was a newer home and bigger than we had before with a banister on the stairs that we kids loved! We would slide down that big old banister and then go outside to play in the backyard. We would ride our tricycles and play with a big red wagon that I had. I would hold the handle back and push with one leg sticking out on the other inside. I remember we had a milkman that came by dressed in all white. He left a couple bottles of milk on the porch. We children would yell, *"The milkman came!"* and momma would say, *"Don't just stand there, bring it in the house."* At this house, we also had a garage which was rare for black people back then. We also had what was called a Pussy Willow tree in front of the house. I remember thinking that it was unique because it had white silky buds that I had never seen before. Stoeple Street was a pretty and peaceful place to live. It had nice lawns and trees which were lined neatly up and down the street. Home was real nice for me then. I would play with my big red wagon or ride my rocking horse upstairs in the house. My school was named Roof Ruff and I can still remember the first time I saw the brick building where I was to go to school. I was so excited. We would have what was called Fun Night at the school and one time my sister Gail and I won a dance contest doing the twist to a Chubby Checker record. Roof Ruff – what a name for a school! We 'burnt' up the floor with our dance moves! At that time my mother and father both had real good jobs-we were doing all right, at least for a while.

Yelling, screaming, fighting – that was my mom and dad; that was something I can remember going on a lot at that time. Although the money was coming in steadily they still fought constantly. He would hit her and they both called each other names – "mother fucker" or "asshole." They drank hard too, almost as hard as they worked. I feel that their drinking had a lot to do with the fighting and arguing but I didn't really understand it at the time. One day my mom and dad got to fighting and my oldest sister Sharon jumped in between them and she cut my dad on the face with a knife. Well, to my surprise, my mom sent Sharon off to juvenile. I could not understand why since Sharon was only trying to defend my mom. The next time I would see my sister would be three years later at a family reunion. Sharon was and still is the best big sister anyone could ever have and I was so excited to see her that day. She never moved back in with us and went on to have her own family but she would come around and check on us when she could.

I remember the family reunion being a really good day for me. It seemed that everybody in my family and the neighborhood came over to my dad and mom's house that day. My grandmother; Granddaddy; aunts; uncles;

cousins; neighbors; and friends were all there and everyone was having a real good time. I remember playing outside with a curly haired boy named Tony who came with my sister Sharon and her boyfriend Charles. We played, ate lots of food, and danced to the music that was really (loud) but nobody complained. Yeah the day was good. But then there came the night.

For some reason Daddy took me and my sister Gail out with him in his 1960 black Chrysler and we had an accident that night? We ran into a tree. He was drinking at that time.

My sister's nose started bleeding a lot and it seemed as if it was not going to stop. Two white women, who we did not know, came up to the car and took us into their house to help. They held *Gail's* head back, pinched her nose, and wiped her face with cold water. I could see everything they were doing through a mirror they had in the room. Finally, the bleeding stopped. When we returned back home everyone had left and the reunion was over. I was so disappointed. That was the end of one of the best days of my life.

While living on Stoeple I had my first experience with death. My older brother Aubrey's grandmother died and we went to view the body. There were other bodies in caskets already at the funeral home when we got there. We had to walk past a few of them to get to my brother's grandmother. While at the funeral home my mother and brother went upstairs to look at caskets and I found myself, at five years old, downstairs with the dead bodies all by myself. I was scared half to death. I ran through the funeral home looking for my mom and finally found her upstairs looking at new caskets with the funeral director. I had nightmares for a long time after that.

3
FROM BAD TO WORSE ON THE EAST SIDE

Around this same time my father left us and in stepped my mother's boyfriend "Lucky." Where did this BASTARD come from? That was all I could think after he got there and stayed for a while. Lucky was real nice to my mother and us kids at first. He bought us ice cream, and almost anything we wanted. We left Stoeple Street and moved to McClellan on the Eastside.

We moved into a four family flat where three other families lived in the other attached units. This was where Lucky first beat up my Mom. *My dad used to beat her up and now another man was going to beat her too?* This is what was on my mind at six years old. I wanted to do whatever I could to stop it and even at this young age, I tried to fight that bastard, but he picked me up and threw me over his back straight on the hard wood floor. It seemed like I saw lighting strike and I was dazed and in pain. After this incident, I felt even more anger towards him and often prayed my mom would leave but it seemed she never would. I don't remember if she ever said anything to him about throwing me to floor like that. She was changing too. Around this same time my mom started using an extension cord when she gave me a beating. When she got mad at me, she would say, *"You're just like your god-damn-daddy, you ain't shit and you ain't never going to be shit!"* I knew that I was in for a long unpleasant haul.

I first learned about sex on this street. Some little girl always wanted to play house under the porch. We would be rubbing up against each other with our clothes on. I laugh every time I think of it now because we thought we were really doing something. There were a lot of nice people living in our neighborhood on McClellan. Still we didn't stay in this neighborhood for long.

4
FRENCH ROAD

Our next house was on French Road, still on the Eastside of Detroit. On French Road is where I learned to ride my first bike. In the beginning, I kept falling off, scarring my knees, and running into trees, but I never gave up. I was so determined to get it right, and I did. I learned to ride that bad boy in one day. I also learned to ride my bike with one hand, and then no hands. That was such a cool accomplishment for me.

It was on French Road that I realized that we were poor and on welfare. There was a white welfare lady that used to drop in on us unannounced. The lady would always ask my mom a lot of personal questions, and would go through all of our things. My momma had to hide everything new, including our clothes, the toaster, and the fact that she had a man living there with us. My mother's boyfriend Lucky had to run out the back door when the welfare lady came so she would not know he was there. Christmas rolled around and this was the first year we got what was called *Goodfellow Boxes*. All of our Christmas presents were in one box. I got one pair of pants, a wool shirt, and some Legos. My little brother got the same, and my two sisters got white baby dolls in their boxes. There weren't any black dolls that we knew of then. What made Christmas great was my mom's cooking. She could really throw down! Chitlins; hog maws; ham; turkey; apple pie; chocolate cake; banana puddin'; sweet potato pies; and the dreaded fruit cake. We also got nuts, and all kinds of fruit. Christmas was a pretty good time for us. My mom would spend all night cleaning chitlins and then she would season them with onions and spices. We would slap some hot sauce on those bad boys and eat them like there was no tomorrow, they were slammin.

One day I woke up to a bunch of loud noise. It turned out Lucky was fighting with my older brother's best friend Lucius. In the fight, Lucky cut him from ear to ear. I was told Lucky had been drinking and got mad when

Lucius called my mother Mom. Maybe he thought Lucius was trying to come on to my mom or something. When I went downstairs blood was everywhere and there were several white towels that had now turned red. Lucius made it to the hospital and lived, but we never saw him again. I felt bad for Lucius and I was hoping the police would take Lucky away for good so we would be rid of him, but the police didn't do a thing to Lucky! That was when I felt something was wrong with the police and I began to distrust them. It seemed like black on black crime didn't matter.

While on French Road I started meeting all kinds of people and making new friends. I remember "Painter", his brother Reesee, and my best friend Esther. Somehow Esther broke her leg and she had to stay in the house for a very long time. I would visit her every day, and we'd talk about all kinds of stuff. I also met older people who became my friends like Mr. Jones at the store around the corner on Warren Street. Mr. Jones got shot one day while someone was robbing his store. Thank God, he lived! Through everything, including the Detroit riots in 1967, Mr. Jones never left the neighborhood. I liked going into his store because he was always nice to me and I felt like he was sincere.

While living on French Road I started my first job. I was so proud, but unfortunately the white man who hired me also fired me the very same day for something I didn't even do. He said that I had started a fire in back of the

store. I didn't even know the first thing about
matches or starting a fire. It was so
disappointing.

We were so poor that sometimes all we
had to eat was mayonnaise, sugar, or syrup
sandwiches. In addition to everything else, we
had to live with Lucky. I often wished that my
momma had any man except for Lucky because
sometimes he was so mean and evil. We didn't
know a lot about this man who my mom brought
into our lives. At one time he was a numbers
runner in the neighborhood. My mom, dad and
granddaddy did regular business with him. He
must have had his eye on my mom all the time
even when my dad was still around. Maybe
something bad in his life made him the way he
was. Or maybe he was just born mean.

One day my Aunt Lillian came over with my new found cousins, Bobby, Brenda, Angie, Sandra, and Kim. I never knew they existed until that day. Aunt Lillian told my mother about a new place we could move into near her and how nice it was. She said it was called Parkside Projects and that we should move there. A month later we were moving again. My brother Craig, my sisters Gail, Judy, and I were so excited!

5
BETTER DAYS IN PARKSIDE PROJECTS

While in the Parkside Projects my dad tried to visit, but my momma wouldn't let him in to see us. I could hear her yelling *"Bastard, get away from here!"* He left and after that, we wouldn't see our dad again for several years.

The projects where we moved were a lot of

25

red brick buildings, with different units located off of Connors and Warren. Both white people and black were living in the same projects at the time. The projects became my playground.

I was all over the place. At first it was a lot of fun. There was a beautiful flower garden across the street with all kinds of flowers where I would often go to hang out. It seemed that when more black people started moving into the neighborhood the flower garden slowly disappeared. Most of the whites moved out and more black people moved in. It seemed like the white management could care less if the black families had anything nice. Not only did the flower garden get less maintenance but after a while the same thing happened with the outdoor playground. In the beginning there was a playground in the middle of the projects, with a swing set, monkey bars, and a sliding board (the whole nine). Everything was almost like new when we moved in, but as time went on, it got worn out and nothing was ever replaced.

We would go over to my Aunt Lillian's house a lot, to visit our new found cousins. We would play outside with two white boys Polly and his brother. Polly and his brother at first tried to befriend us and tried to amuse us by eating worms. They would also steal their mother's money and give it to us. They said she didn't know and they could get into her purse without her knowing.

Because we were so poor, we had to be creative. When it snowed, it snowed heavy in Detroit, one year the snow got up to three feet. We would have snowball fights by balling up the snow and throwing it at each other and we would also make sleds out of cardboard to slide down hills. We thought we were living well because it was fun as kids. At Parkside I met my first girlfriend, Toni. We called ourselves boyfriend and girlfriend, even though we were both so young.

One of my worst days happened while I was living in the projects. My granddaddy Alex Sangster died. I loved my granddaddy. He used to take me everywhere, and would always buy me Cracker Jacks with the real prizes in them - like the magnifying glass, poppers, and the games where you would pull the handle and the little ball would move around the maze. My granddaddy was very special to me. He and his two brothers came from Ripley, Tennessee. He worked hard for several days a week at the

Chrysler Motor Company in Detroit. At the end

of each day he liked to drink his shot of bourbon

and on the weekend he loved riding around in

his black Chrysler - just visiting people. They

laid his body out for viewing at a place called

Swanson funeral home which was off of East

Grand Boulevard and Mack. Most of the black

people went to Swanson's when somebody died

back then. The loss of my granddaddy was a

very sad time in my life, my memories of him will

be with me always.

6
A NEW LEASE ON LIFE –
ST. CLAIR STREET

My mother's boyfriend Lucky would still

come around while we were in the projects. He

was never a totally permanent fixture. He was

still drinking and beating up on my momma

when he got drunk. She was still taking it. That

is why I was so shocked and I couldn't believe it

when he bought a house on St. Clair Street and

my mom actually moved us in with him. No matter what we kids thought, he wasn't going away and we spent a lot of our childhood years on St. Clair.

Around 1963 the Eastside of Detroit was a nice area for Colored people as we were called back then. I met one of my friends for life, Ricky while walking home from my new elementary school Hutchinson one day. Come to find out we both lived on St. Clair Street. Back then we would buy all kinds of candy for a penny from any corner store, Squirrels, Tootsie Rolls, Mary Janes, you name it-we could get it! We would take a little brown paper bag to school full of candy and try to hide it from the teachers. When they caught us eating candy, they would take it. We tried our best to hide our candy but they would often find it. If we got caught doing something wrong back then, our teachers would paddle us. One teacher would put holes in his paddles to spread the pain around. He even had the nerve to name his two paddles, "Mr. and Mrs. Cool." One day a teacher tried to paddle me, and I told her *"My momma said not to hit me, but to send me home."* When I got home my mom beat the piss out of me with an extension cord while I was butt naked. If I could take it back, I would have chosen the paddle. My favorite things at school were playing tag on the playground and picking at the girls.

I couldn't believe it when our new school turned out to be off of French Road. We were back in the old hood. I got into many fights at my new elementary school. I believe kids picked on me because I was so small. It seemed like I had to fight every day. While in class someone would say "I'm going to beat you up when school is out." I tried sneaking out of a side door or two, but they were blocked by other kids who wanted to see a fight. Once outside the other kids that wanted to see a fight would circle around me and the other person, the fight was on. I was over powered most of the time. Somebody would get me on the ground, and I would say "I give up." After giving up the fight was over. Early in my life I took a lot of ass whippings, but the older I got the more that changed. I was the one who started kicking ass. I would seldom back down from a fight.

St. Clair started out innocent. I met a lot

of new friends that I would have for life. We used to play tag, hide and go seek, and chase each other with cap guns until the street lights came on. When the street lights came on we could hear our mother yelling and she would call each of us by our name – *"Beannie, Gail, Judy, and Craig, get in this house!"* You would also hear all the other mothers yelling for their kids to get in the house. Everyone would be running in different directions.

We had what we called blocks in Detroit, and our block was St. Clair. During Christmas the streets were so beautiful with white snow. Every house on the street was decorated with lights. So much took place on St. Clair and in our neighborhood that I don't know where to begin. All of the adults were my extended parents, Mr. and Mrs. Daniels, Mr. and Mrs. White, Mr. and Mrs. Beasley, Mr. Herman and Mrs. Perkins, and so many others. If they caught you doing something wrong, they would either spank your butt themselves or tell your parents on you. There was also Reggie and Rose who were two of my dearest friends who really surprised me when they got together and married one another. They were like a big brother and big sister to me. The people on my block became my St. Clair family. One of my best friends, Tim, moved in on St. Clair after I did. He, Ricky, and I, bonded right away. We also had several bullies on our street. Two in particular were Rome and Danny. They used to hang us upside down from trees. One day Tim, Ricky, and I got Rome back for some of his antics by playing a prank on him. We told him

that we were going to Edge Water Park and
asked if he wanted to go along. Of course he
did. As we were heading out, each of us made
up some lie about having to leave and go do
something real quick and we would meet back
up with him at the bus stop, but we simply were
going around the corner to hide from him. He
went on and we lost him for a while. We went
and sat on Mrs. Daniels porch for about half an
hour. Rome finally figured out that we were
pulling a prank on him, and he came around the
corner fuming saying, *"Y'all just don't come my
way, just don't come my way!"* We all burst out
laughing and laughed until we almost cried. He
just kept walking and went into his house which
wasn't far from where we were. It must have
had an effect on him because after that day he
stopped bullying us and tried to be friends. We

accepted him into our group and would all hang out together. He actually became one of our best friends. I got into many fights with some of the other neighborhood bullies and soon found out it was simply best to avoid them than fight all the time.

While on St. Clair I loved drawing pictures and writing songs. There was a lot of talent in the neighborhood. It's strange how so many talented children's dreams can be destroyed by their environment. We were developing a sense of pride and unity about ourselves as black people and then that was replaced by an influx of drugs, gang violence, prostitution, alcohol abuse, pimps, and partying. I feel that a lot of this came from blacks being exploited by movies like "Super Fly" where drugs were portrayed as cool in this movie, "The Mack" where pimping was simply another means of getting rich, and "Come Back Charleston Blue" which portrayed ripping off people as a way of getting ahead. Sometimes in the end the crooks got what they deserved and were brought down by their own people or the police. The messages sent were often negative but still were seen by many of us as a cool way of life although it was a wrong way to live. These movies were coming out one after the other and we were caught up in watching them and sometimes we were convinced that what they portrayed was true. We had not heard of exploitation at the time or knew that many of these movies were having a big influence on our lives and neighborhoods. There were also other movies I have to mention that became my all time favorites – "Cooley High",

"Uptown Saturday Night", and "Shaft."

Money or the lack thereof, was also a big problem at my house, and many others. My mother was paying most of her life on some cheap furniture that she bought from a Jewish furniture store in the neighborhood. Whenever she was late with a payment they had so many extra fees and interest rate hikes added on that she could never actually pay it off. A lot of businesses were in the hood but not many, if any, were black owned. When many of the blacks could not pay their rent or house notes they would be kicked out and the process would start over with another black family. Many tried but few seemed to be able to actually get ahead in our neighborhood or not have to struggle for everything they got. I remember hearing my mom and some of her friends talk about what was going on but there was little they could do financially. These things brought a lot of acute pain, suffering, distress, and other problems into our communities that still exist today.

While on St. Clair I started drinking and smoking weed (marijuana) at an early age; I believe that I was around twelve. I wanted to escape my environment, and to be cool like the people in the movies. I also was trying to fit in with the people around me. I even started stealing around this time from a store called Spartans Atlantics off of Warren and Conners. I had to do something since nobody was trying to help me with my raggedy clothes or the holes in my shoes which I had to cover up with cardboard. A con man named "Shugga" would have me, my friends Ricky and Tim along with some of my brother Craig friends go downtown and pretend to be in a boys club called the Boys Blue Ribbons Club and we would con people for money. We did it because we were young and gullible, and because we wanted some money in our pockets. Shugga gave us clip boards with white paper money holders and we clipped them to the board where we could put the quarters, dimes, nickels, and pennies into each slot as we received them and as one filled up we could switch it out with another one. We kept the paper bills in our pockets. He also gave us some cheap looking different color ink pins to sell as well. Our agreement was to ask for money and sell as many pens as we could for a designated time each day and then meet back up with him at a particular spot. We would spread out all over town and ask people if they would like to donate or buy a pen and help us go to summer camp? At the end of the day each person gave him $15.00 and we could keep the rest. I pulled in fifty dollars one day. He would then drop us back off on our side of town. Believe it or not he would sometimes take us home in a limousine and we would all be crowed in the back. We thought that was the coolest thing ever and that he was the man. Whenever we rolled into the neighborhood in that limousine it made us more willing to go out and con more people the next day. He made us feel special in order to keep using us. After a while he got busted for that and a laundry list of other hustles he had going on and I heard he went to jail for a while.

When we needed bikes, we would go out to

what we called the white suburb, and take the little white kids bikes. They always had the best ones and seemed so much more privileged than we were. It was easy back then to get into and out of the neighborhoods at night as long as we avoided the big four. The big four were four white cops riding in the same car four deep and when they caught black people doing whatever, they would often threaten us and beat us up with their black Billy clubs. Word on the streets was they would often beat people for no reason. Someone told me that they would take you into an alley and beat you in the stomach because it wouldn't leave any marks.

Ricky and I would smoke a few joints and have a few beers but my friend Tim would only drink one beer. He couldn't drink much without getting blasted. We would round up some of the neighborhood girls and some more of the fella's and head out to the house parties. My sister Judy, her best friend Peewee (Tiwanna), and another friend Janette would often go with us as well. It seemed someone was always having a party at their house. At these parties, the people in our neighborhoods would be doing all kinds of dances like, the Funky Chicken, the Bump, and the Four Corners. When I look back on it the Funky Chicken was funny and way out there because we actually flapped our arms and legs around like we were chickens and thought we were really getting down. My friend Pee Wee was one of the baddest (best) dancer's I ever saw. When the Robot came out, she danced it to where she would robot over to an imaginary car, lean over, take an imaginary key out of her pocket, open the door, get in the car and crank it up, doing the Robot the whole time. I had never seen anything like it. Years later when I saw Michael Jackson do the Robot the first thing I thought was he didn't have anything on my friend Pee Wee. Black people in Detroit and around the country were coming up with these dances on our own.

"Back in the day", as they say now, we had some of the best music on 45's and 33's (LP's). I started catching the D.S.R. bus downtown at an early age, taking in movies, concerts and whatever. One of my most memorable moments was when my sister Gail and I caught the bus downtown to the Fox Theater to see what was called the Motown Revue. We got to see, Little Stevie

Wonder, The Supremes, The Temptations, Smokey Robinson & The Miracles, Willie and Lester, Martha Reeves and the Vandellas, Gladys Knight and the Pips, Ike and Tina Turner, Marvin Gaye, and so many other acts, just for two dollars! It's hard to believe huh! When I found out a black man named Berry Gordy was behind all of this, I was so proud. I also went to a place in downtown Detroit called Cobo Hall to see the Funkadelics, Parliament, and Chaka Khan and Rufus. It seemed all of us kids in Detroit were trying to emulate these acts.

We were really having a good time on St. Clair, but my mom and Lucky were still drinking and acting like fools. Mom finally decided to move and leave Lucky after he shot at her one night with a 30-30 Winchester rifle. They had been arguing and by the sound of it we all knew it was time to split. My mom and all of us headed for the door. I heard the sound of the riffle going off and turned back to look just as my mom tripped and fell to the ground. She had tripped going down the steps. If she had not fallen in that instant he would have shot her in the back. Thank God he missed! She got up and we kept on running as fast as scared little rabbits.

Well despite all that, we moved only a few blocks over to Hurlbut Street. We were away from my mom's boyfriend Lucky, and again thank God! At least Lucky was gone, for now.

7
BACK IN THE HOOD ON HURLBUT STREET

My mom and all four of us kids moved into a small shotgun house on Hurlbut Street. You could literally walk through the front door and practically be walking right out the back door of this house. That's why it was called "Shotgun."

Once again I had to make new friends and I met many people over here too including

"Hands", "Dex", "Geno", "White Boy Bill" and many others along with their families. Of course we called Bill "White Boy Bill" because he and his family were one of the only few whites left in the neighborhood.

Hurlbut was still in the hood. On Hurlbut Street things really escalated in terms of how our lives would be shaped in the hood. All of us kids in the neighborhood would fight a lot - each other and anyone else. To us it was just a normal part of our upbringing. One of my main friends and foes was Dex. We would fight almost every day but we also would hang out from time to time. Sometimes I'd win the fight and sometimes he would win. Dex was the one who taught me how to skip school, and how to steal wine from the store. We both would walk in and one of us would do something to distract the person at the counter, while the other would walk out with the wine. We thought nothing of getting drunk or going out to look for someone to jack up for their money.

On Hurlbut an ordinary day for us kids would be raiding fruit trees, stealing garbage can tops to use for shields, going out to vacant lots and, having pear fights, or following the dare devil "White Boy Bill" by climbing garages, and jumping from garage to garage. We would also hang from the tops of vacant houses, and jump to the ground. I cut my hand real bad one day by jumping from a house. I had to walk several blocks to Dr. Leach's office, the neighborhood doctor. He did a great job on my hand. Everybody in the community went to Dr.

Leach. He was the first black doctor I had ever encountered. Despite getting hurt occasionally, we would hop trains, and run through the graveyard at night. Everyday there was some drama. We would be fighting, shooting craps, snatching purses, breaking in houses, throwing things off the expressway, or stealing off the potato chip truck. I believe they started putting the gates around the bridges on the expressway, and locking the potato chip trucks up because of us kids. While on Hurlbut, my sisters Gail and Judy taught me how to smoke cigarettes. They said *"Just smoke it like a joint."* I was sick for about a day, but after that I was smoking like a professional. I learned to French inhale, making perfectly symmetrical smoke rings under my nose. I really thought I had it going on.

While living on Hurlbut there was an older white man named Mr. Broadnax who became angry with some of us one day and said to us, *"Why don't you niggers go back to Africa where ya'll come from?"* Of course we didn't take that lightly. In Detroit we called the night before Halloween Devil's Night, and we would get people back that we didn't like. We burnt down Mr. Broadnax's garage. It seemed like white people would always start some shit, and blame blacks just to have an excuse to move out of the neighborhood. He left and the number kept dwindling.

I was around thirteen when I got my first piece of real pussy as we called it. This girl named Gwen snuck me through her parent's back door while they were asleep. We had sex on an old couch in their basement. Afterwards she snuck me back out. I got my first nut as we called it in those days and I went home happier than ever. Gwen couldn't have been more than a year older than me, maybe fourteen. In those days it was a badge of honor to get a girl, but if you told you would never get her again. I was so excited I didn't just tell one person, I told everybody. That was it for me and Gwen. After Gwen, I chased behind everything in a skirt and was often successful.

White Boy Bill had become one of my best friends, until one day his older brother accused me of messing with their sister Dee. I didn't touch that girl! White Boy Bill's brother threatened me and I vowed to get him back. In our neighborhoods several gangs were starting up at the time and many attempted to pattern themselves after some of the real black gangsters in Detroit who presented a professional image, dressed real sharp in Sharkskin suits, Dobbs, Knox, and Borsalino hats, Longines watches, Alligator shoes, Thick and Thin Socks, and silk underwear. Even though they looked real sharp they didn't mind roughing someone up or taking them completely out. One night my sister Gail was having a yard party, and a little dude named "Gee Chee" and I was talking. Gee Chee was a part of one of the up and coming gangs at that time the BA's (Black Avengers). He also stuttered when he talked. During one of our conversations he asked me *"Yeah Beannie man, An-n-n-nybody been messing with you man? An-n-n-nybody's been mes-s-s-ing with you?"* I said *"Yeah, the white boy across the street."* At that point he just lost it! He yelled out *"BA'S! BA'S! It* was like he was sending out a distress call. I saw a big dude named Norman chop a board in half that my sister had across the gate, and about fifty other dudes ran out the yard and they all headed over to White Boy Bill's house. They beat up his whole family, including his dad. After this incident, Bill and his family moved. This was the first time that I became familiar with gang action. It seemed that after this occurred I became more aware of gangs in the neighborhood and others began to spring up. A gang popped up on my old street calling themselves the Latin Playboys even though not one of them was Latin. I believe a dude named Peanut started this gang. Most of the Latin Playboys were my old friends. Years later the

Latin Playboys and the Black Avengers joined together and became the Black Killers (BK's). My brother Craig joined the gang and I believe he had something to do with giving the BK'S their name. Somebody burned down Bill's family's house after they moved. A friend named Ross taught my other friends and me how to pitch money and shoot dice in White Boy Bill's old backyard. We called Ross leaner Ross because when we pitched pennies that joker would often toss his penny and it would lean right up against the wall. That was something to see. He would take all of our money. Yeah, you really have to be a good penny pitcher to make that penny lean as often as he did.

One day my sister turned me on to a drug called "pee", we called it a penny cap because it sold for a dollar. In Detroit we could cop drugs

from almost anywhere. Whenever I wanted

some drugs I would walk up to a dope house

and ask for some drugs. The dope dealer would

ask "who sent you?" I would give a friend's

name, and then he would let me cop some dope.

We would snort this stuff up our noses. Later

on in my life I found out that I was snorting

heroin. While living on Hurlbut, my sister Gail,

some of her friends, and I would go to a place

called the Psychedelic. It was a house party off

of French Road across the bridge. A man named

Mr. Goins used to give it and he charged us fifty

cents to get in. Everybody was at the

Psychedelic. The music was blasting and he

sold beer. There were posters on the walls, a

strobe light flashing all over the place, and a

blue fluorescent light along with it. We all

looked blue and like we were moving in slow motion. We had a ball going to the Psychedelic every weekend, with one exception – a fight always broke out after the party. Despite that, it was a real cool place to be. I had a gun put to my head at least twice at these parties. One time for trying to talk to another dudes girl and the other was when one of the dudes who was throwing a party thought I was actually trying to fight one of the girls at the party but as it turned out she and I were really friends and we were only play fighting. He didn't realize this at the time and I guess he called himself trying to be bad. She explained to him what was going on and he cooled down. Having a gun put to my head was – not so cool, but thank God it wasn't tragic. I'd be at a party drinking, dancing, and having a good time. Too often after the party I would be so drunk that I could hardly function. At one time or two a lady wanted to take me home with her, she turned me down because I was too drunk. One night I was so high that I hit at least five parked cars while driving. My friend Mo use to say "Allen a drunk ain't shit." He was right, from my experiences, I'd tell anyone to stay away from the abuse of drugs and alcohol.

Well like I said a lot of stuff took place on Hurlbut. Yeah, once again, Lucky started coming around and as usual for some strange reason my momma decided to move back in with him after all that had gone down between them. They moved us back to St. Clair Street. Our lives had become like a revolving door.

Friends for life!

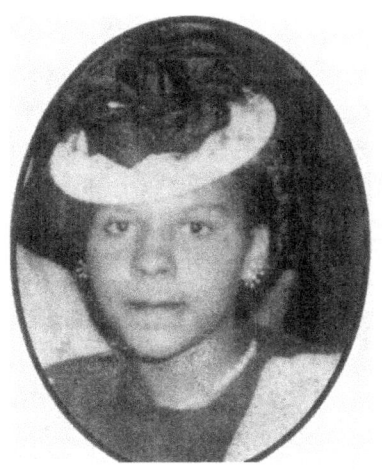

Hallie Sangster my beloved mom.

Aubrey Sangster a smooth and intelligent big brother.

My sister Gail, she was always a Class Act.

My sister Judy, she is a beautiful African American blonde.

Alex Sangster my Grand Daddy. He spent a lot of time with me and I thank him for that.

My sister Sharon, she is the loving and protective big sister.

Craig Allen my little brother whom I miss greatly.

Aubrey, Big Momma, Cool Rick, and Woodson III, were relaxing outside in Detroit.

Big Momma, My loving grandmother was one of the people who taught me about God.

Me and Jackie on our wedding day!

My sons, Woodson Allen III and Lamar Allen are two handsome dudes. This is an earlier picture of them.

That's me. Young and free at fifteen years old!

This is me, Army proud.

8
REVERSE, REVERSE, BACK TO ST.CLAIR

Well, much hadn't changed on this street with the exception that everyone was growing up real fast. All of us liked going to the Admiral Theater to watch Godzilla and King Kong. Around this same time we got our first color television. I enjoyed watching Bat Man and Robin and The Green Hornet and Kato

where Kato turned out to be Bruce Lee. Man he
was kicking ass and taking names as we would
say back then. My brother, my sister's, and I
would also sit in front of the TV and watch Soul
Train so we could learn the latest dance moves
and see our favorite entertainers. We were all
partying and getting into the Jackson
Five. There was a club on Warren called the 007
where there was a talent contest every week. A
group which called themselves the Fairview Five,
that patterned themselves after the Jackson
Five, would win almost every week. Everybody
wanted to be like the J'5 so they could get all the
ladies. We were all wearing afros, bellbottom
pants, blazer jackets, and platform shoes. One
day I decided to change my afro to a process
with finger waves. I was as cool as ever. We
also liked to go to the ice cream parlor off of

Warren and St. Clair. Mr. Chad had some of the best hard lemon, strawberry, and vanilla ice cream that you would ever want to eat! He also made the best banana splits in the world.

While living back on St. Clair I also remember we had this bad little dog named Betsy. She bit the mailman one time and the real shocker about her for me came when she ate all of her own puppies. That really blew my mind. I also remember being up on Warren Street one day and someone had shot a man and blew his brains out. I didn't actually see him get shot, but I did see his brains lying in the street. The cars were running over his brains like nothing and just kept on going. I looked at this for a while, and then headed back home; I was in shock. I told everybody about what I saw and they couldn't believe it. They were stunned by the awful news and that I actually saw all of this.

A few days later my two friends Ricky, Tim, and I stole a wagon to make a go car. We stole the spray paint from Aubrey's house, my brother. We went over to Rome's house that day. For some reason the paint wouldn't come out of the can so I started beating on it with a pipe and the can blew up in my face. I started yelling *"Rome put it out!"* He ran and got the hose it was on (none other than) jet spray. Things went from bad to worse because that water tore a lot of my skin completely off. At this point I was in absolute pain. Mrs. Robinson took me down to her basement, and put some towels on me. When my older brother Aubrey heard about what had happened, he came speeding around the corner like a mad man and took me to the doctor's office. The doctor gave me a salve to put on my skin every day. I laid up at my brother Aubrey, his wife Pat, (who was like a big sister to me) and their son Bubbles house for a couple of weeks while I healed. Man! All kinds of relatives and friends were coming to see me, and bringing me all kinds of good things. They brought me ice cream, cards, fruit, and get well wishes.

Well, I got better and was still as crazy as ever when I returned home to St. Clair Street. My sister Gail and some of her girlfriends bet me five dollars and a pack of cigarettes that I couldn't drink half a gallon of Slow Gin Fizz straight, without stopping. I took them up on their bet and won. Afterwards when that buzz started kicking in, I thought that was the end of me. It was like I went from sober to straight drunk all at once. My head was spinning and I could barely stand up. My friend Bobo's dad, Mr. Johnson said *"Give that boy some butter, and have him to keep walking, or else he is going to die."* I ate the butter, and then walked around two long blocks for about two hours – it seemed like forever. I was still drunk as hell, but I pulled through and after that I was straight. I continued doing one crazy thing after another. *I* still had a whole heap of growing up to do.

By this time it seemed that almost all of our sense of black pride and black power had all but disappeared. There was one exception in my life though, and that was Mrs. Hanks who lived on Hurlbut. She had in her possession one of the first pictures of a black Jesus that I had ever seen. It was hard for me to conceive in my mind that Jesus could be of a dark race after seeing a white Jesus on my mother's and everybody else's wall for so long. A picture of a white Jesus was even on the walls in some black churches. I have to admit it really got me to thinking and realizing that Jesus could be of another race, even mine. I believe that thought planted an early seed of transformation in my life.

9
SCOTTDALE GEORGIA

One day my uncle, his wife, and my cousin Donna came to see us. I was across the street playing catch with one of my best friends, James, when my sister Judy came over to me saying, *"Hurry up and come to the house somebody wants to see you."* I said, *"Who?"* She said, *"Come on, it's a surprise."* It turned out to be one of the biggest surprises of my life. It was my dad's brother. We talked for a while and then he asked me *"Would you like to come down*

south?" I said *"Yes."* He said he would send for
me and I could go there and meet some more of
my family. He said my dad was there and he
would surprise him with a visit from me. I was
excited and wondered if he would keep his word
but he did. He sent me some clothes and my
older sister Sharon bought me some silk
underwear. The next thing that I knew, I was on
a Greyhound bus on my way to Atlanta, Georgia.
It was a long and uneventful bus ride. This trip
was the first time I had ever left Detroit. I looked
out of the bus window and I couldn't believe the
view. Traveling through the south was so
beautiful. When I arrived in Georgia my uncle
picked me up from the bus station. I was so
excited to see him but all I could think about
was seeing my dad again and what my new
experience would be like? My uncle was also a

minister and he took me to his church the first night I got there. While at his church he was arguing with a white man about something in the Bible. I could not believe what had just happened. My uncle was actually arguing with the man, in church. That struck me as really strange. But what actually happened at the church really didn't matter; all that was on my mind was seeing my dad after so many years. After church my uncle took me to Scottsdale, Georgia to see my dad. My dad lived in a housing complex and when I got to my dad's house I was so excited and a little nervous too because I had not seen him for so long. He welcomed me with open arms, hugged me, and said *"Hey son."* He had a big smile on his face and was genuinely happy to see me. I was also happy to see him. After my dad welcomed me, my beautiful stepmom who I called my second mom hugged me and welcomed me in. She said she didn't want me to call her by her name, but I was to call her mom. I also met some of my other family members who were my brothers and sisters, Sarah, Teresa, Clifton, Charley, Tosh, and Ronnie. They all showed me plenty of love. I had yet to meet three other sisters, Katherine, Hattie, and Nan. Seeing these relatives brought back a memory of when my grandfather on my dad's side once brought some of my sisters to Detroit to meet us when we were very young. We played together and they would slide down our big old banister with me and the rest of my siblings. My family is intertwined with many brothers and sisters and we all considered each other as such. We all would say there is no such thing as step brother's or step sisters in this family. We were all just one big family. They were all just as loving and accepting as my dad, mom, and the rest of my family. I never knew how much I had in common with my Georgia brothers and sisters. Most of them liked to party and have fun just as much as I did, if not more. I felt like I was at home, I even called Scottsdale my little Detroit.

Because my uncle was a minister he felt I should stay with him so that he could take me to church and see that I hung around what he considered respectable individuals at his church. I believe in his own way he was trying to do some sort of intervention for me and was trying to get me to walk the straight and narrow while I was in Georgia. Because they were brothers and my uncle was responsible for bringing my dad and me back together after so many years, my dad said it would be ok with him if I stayed with my uncle while I was in town but I could come back and forth to see him. He thought it would be good for me and at first so did I. Well, my uncle took me back to his house, and I was as bored as ever! I tried to settle down and be content there but I was restless and anxious to get back to hanging in the streets and just being me. One day I asked my uncle to buy me some All Star shoes (Chuck Taylors). Apparently he was not into the fashions of the time and thought all-stars were simply shoes with stars all over them because that is exactly what he bought me, a pair of no name shoes that were red, white, and blue, covered with stars. I said to him *"These are not All-*

Stars", and he said *"Yes they are, look at all the stars."* I didn't know whether to laugh or cry. From that moment on, I knew it was time for me to leave his house! I knew he was not getting where I was coming from and I really wasn't trying to understand where he was going. I immediately called my dad and asked if I could come to Scottsdale and stay with them? He didn't hesitate and said *"Come on."*

I can't begin to describe how much I enjoyed living with my Georgia family. They showed me so much love and respect, that it changed my whole outlook about life. We were always partying and having fun. At Christmas my second *mom* gave me a present along with everyone else, a pair of socks. She always gave us socks and we loved it. She cooked a big dinner and boy she could really throw down. She

cooked just like my mom in Detroit. This
Christmas was very special but it was not the
highlight of my night. The highlight of my night
was when my brother-in-law Sam and my sister
Nan brought this girl named Shena over to meet
me. We clicked right off the bat and I thought I
had met the love of my life. My brother Clifton
who was around my age, introduced me to many
other people like my cousin "Pooch", my main man
"Rab", "Toot, Boone", and two of my favorite
cousins, Vicky and Tobbie, just to name a few. I
only stayed in Georgia for a few months and then I
returned to Detroit. Those few months in Georgia
were some of the best months of my life and I was
happy. I returned to Detroit with a different
outlook on life. I knew where my dad was and had
spent time with him, my second mom, and my
other brothers and sisters, the southern
hospitality was real!

10
REALITY CHECK

No sooner than I had returned to Detroit, I sadly received a 'Dear John' letter from what I thought was the love of my life, Shena. I'll never forget what it said, *"Once upon a time you knocked upon my daydream door, and I gently said come in, then reality came along and said it was nice having you here, but it's nicer having you there."* I was surprised and got real upset about it because this was the first time my heart was broken. Unfortunately, it wouldn't be the last. I had many girlfriends after Shena but for some reason I could never seem to find the right one for me.

There wasn't much that had changed in Detroit while I was away. The battle continued. I had to get on with life and survive the best way I could. Ricky, Tim, me, and the rest of my friends were all still kicking it. We were growing into our own real fast!

Well like I said, I was back in Detroit at this point and armed with a pistol that I had stolen from my uncle down south, and an iron pipe that I had wrapped up with electrical tape. I had my *stepdad* Lucky's name written all over these things. I was going to kill Lucky, or he was going to kill me! He and my mom were still fighting and I was trying to jump in and stop it when I was around but it was getting to be too much. I had planned to catch Lucky off guard and shoot him, or crack his head to the white meat but I could never get him at the right moment. At this point I was not scared of him anymore and really wanted to mess him up, but I had to be real with the situation because if I didn't finish the job he would be on the hunt for me. Things with Lucky slowed to a simmer for a while as it would often do, but I was always on the lookout for a chance to get him and was simply biding my time.

I still wasn't doing much with my life in Detroit, besides running the streets and partying. One night my friend Ricky and I went to this house party a block over on Harding Street. Everybody was having a good time, shooting the breeze, drinking, listening to the music and kicking it with the ladies. Late into the party, all the ladies left, except one. For some stupid reason all of us dudes started pulling out our guns and showing them off. I had a small derringer pistol that only carried two rounds; everybody else had bigger guns and many I had not seen before. Near the end of the party my friend Ricky grabbed the one girl who was there by the hand and asked her to dance. She said *"Yes"*, and when she stood up she somehow fell over the end of the couch. The dude whose house we were partying at saw her stumble and yelled at Ricky, *"Don't be grabbing her like that, or else I'm going to kick your ass!"* Of course I jumped in and said *"You're not going to do anything to him!"* I showed my gun. Then the dude said *"Wait a minute, I've got something to double what you've got"* he started

going up the basement stairs and then made a

right up some more stairs. Ricky and I went up

the stairs to the left toward the side door to

exit. For some reason I turned around and

busted a cap in the dude's direction as we were

exiting and he was hit. Ricky and I

started hauling ass out of there. We ran

through the alley jumped a fence and was

running through this yard when two white cops

yelled for us to stop. We tried to act like we

didn't hear them at first so I could get rid of the

gun and they yelled for us to stop again. I

ditched the gun in some bushes and we stopped,

turned around and walked back towards the

cops. When we met up with them they asked

"What are you fuckers running from?" I said

"Some big boys are chasing us." One of them

said to us *"You fuckers got good sense to stop when the police tell you to stop?"* We said *"Yes sir."* The other cop then said *"You fuckers get on your way"*, and we turned around and kept hauling ass.

After the shooting incident we hid out for about two weeks over at Ricky's dad's place on Rose Lawn on the Westside. We were both out of school for the summer so it was easy for us to stay out of sight. Ricky and I finally came out of hiding and word on the street was that I had only skinned the dude, but he was looking for us and said he was going to break both of my arms and one of Ricky's. It was also said that some little boy found the pistol in the area where I had thrown it and had somehow shot off a finger. I felt bad about that. Fortunately things died down over the incident with the dude and the kid or so I thought. One night while I was walking over to my friend Tim's house , these two dudes drove up on me and starting yelling that's him. They parked the car so fast I could hear the tires squeal. I recognized them as being friends with the guy I had shot at the party and they each had a machete looking knife in their hand. With my upbringing, win or lose, I didn't normally back down from a fight, but with no weapon on me, and these two dudes holding those knives, I knew I had to make a quick exit. I took off running as fast as I could and they came after me. My heart was pounding and in my mind I was telling myself don't go in any alley you can't get out of. I knew the neighborhood well and I was dodging and weaving but they were pretty fast too. I knew if they caught me I would get messed up or even killed. I looked up and saw my friend Tim's house and ran up on his porch. His sister Kay was outside and wanted to know what the hell was going on and she saw the two dudes coming up. All I could get out of my mouth was "they are after me." Kay was a pretty girl but she was tough and didn't take any mess. She got in front of me and as the guy's ran into the yard she said in a commanding voice "y'all can just turn around right now because nobody is going to mess with Beannie." One of them said that little punk shot off a gun at our party and hit our friend and he almost hit us too. Kay said she didn't know what went down there but nothing was going down over here tonight and they had best get on up off her property. Then one said "that punk better apologize for what he did." I think at this point they respected that she was bold and standing up for me, and I don't think they could be sure whether or not if she had anything on her to back up her talk, and they decided to let it slide with just an apology from me, so I said "it's cool man, I didn't mean nothing, I'm sorry for what I did." It was like a standoff and then the other one said, "Let's roll" to his friend and they turned around, went back to their car, and drove off. I was shaking inside but I didn't try to show it. I stayed at Tim's house for a little while and then left. Of course I had to explain everything to Kay and I thanked her for standing up for me. I also thanked God for not letting things go any further and that Kay was home that day. I will never forget what she did for me and how it all worked out. I stayed away from house parties for a while and things died down over the incident. I began to relax and life returned to normal. Only one other time did I see the dude I shot, and that was when I was on his street one day and un-expectantly I ran into him. I immediately thought something would jump off between us, but he didn't do or say Jack shit! I said what's up and he simply looked at me and said nothing. We both just kept on stepping. Even with the situation of the kid finding the gun there was never anything pointing to me or any other stories about it so I think that was only a rumor, but boy was that ever a reality check!

Lucky got to arguing with my mother again and I stepped to Lucky, and said *"I'm tired of you jumping on my mom, and arguing with her all the time."* He went off, and said *"I do all I can for you mother fuckers. You can get the fuck out of my house!"* At this point I was older, sixteen, and really didn't care what he said as long as he didn't put his hands on me. In the back of my mind I wanted him to just do something to make me get my gun and my pipe and end this constant bad situation. I just kept mouthing off at him and to my surprise he didn't touch me. I know my mother heard us but she didn't try to stop us. He left the room and didn't come back in, and I felt victorious. We made it through a couple of nights but the tension was always there. Lucky and I kept going at each other verbally for two days but I was always cautious. I felt he was plotting something against me. I knew well enough he wasn't taking this back talk lightly and he must have said something to my mom because she came to

me one day when I was outside and sat down on
the front porch with me. She called over some
older dude named Ray from across the street. She
asked him to tell me about Job Corps. Apparently
someone had told Ray about it and my mom
thought it would be something good for me to do at
the time. Ray said, *"Beannie, man it's cool you can
get a trade and your high school diploma".* At first I
didn't know what the hell he was talking about,
but from his excitement I said to myself, it has to
be better than this hell hole. I signed up the next
day and in two weeks I was ready to go to Job
Corps in Kentucky. My mom allowed my family,
and my friends to throw a going away party for
me. "Boocoo" people showed up and we partied
like this was our last night to ever see each other
again. Lucky partied with us and acted like he
was real happy. I know he was happy to see me go
and I was glad to be going.

11
LIFE CHANGING TURNS IN THE ROAD

When I arrived on the scene at Job Corps I was put into a dorm. There were four dorms, and we had names for them all, Ace, Duce, Tray, and Ghetto. Most of the dudes in Job Corps that I met were from Chicago. They were mostly Yellowstone and Blackstone Rangers, gang members. One of their sayings was *"Bow down nigger, Chi love."* Even then the "N" word was being used. We didn't think anything about using it then. I was like *"Yeah, right Detroit bow down!"* This didn't go over very well. I often had to fight to defend myself but it did toughen me up and made me a little stronger mentally and physically. Job Corps did feed us pretty good, and we received a fifteen dollar check every two weeks for personals. After about six months we got a stipend and our instructors took us to buy a few clothes, and I mean only a few. I still have a picture where I am wearing one of the shirts I bought back then. Most of the people I met in Job Corps were from what I call rough backgrounds like me and they fought, gambled, sold dollar joints, got high by snorting glue, partied, and everything else. Most of the time I thought they were from Detroit because we had so much in common but the majority of them was from the West and South side of Chi-town (Chicago). I had one good friend in particular who we called John Boy. We hung out and partied a lot. He and I were both popular with the ladies when we went out. We would often hang out on the weekends. John Boy and I would drink a bottle of Wild Irish Rose wine, smoke a couple of joints, and hang outside of the female dorm at the nearby college trying to scoop some ladies. In Job Corps they made both of us leaders along with another dude we called Big Man. We received some badges and got tough with anyone who broke the rules. I had signed up for a trade in welding when I first came into Job Corps and I finished my welding course after ten months and received a certificate. My instructors were good people like Mrs. Bailey who taught math, and Mr. Jarvis, my welding instructor. They were both so

patient and kind to me. In addition to taking

the class and getting a certificate we also had to

pass a welding test and get certified. If we

passed the certification test this could mean a

good job and maybe a lifetime opportunity to

make money and be independent. Not to

mention helping our families out financially. I

was real excited about this chance. After we

received our certificates we traveled to Ingle's

ship yard in Mississippi to take the test. Out of

ten of us who took the test only two of us

passed, and I wasn't one of the two. Man I was

disappointed. I felt like a failure after going

through all I went through and still not passing

the test. I wanted it so badly because it was an

opportunity for me to make it on my own and

have a skill I could rely on other than running

the streets. There was still another opportunity for us to get training until we passed the test, but it required us having to stay longer in Mississippi and Job Corps was not paying for that. I was already running out of money, so I took my certificate and ended up back in Georgia for a brief stint with my dad and my second mom. I was supposed to get an extra check from Job Corps for about two hundred and fifty dollars which they sent to my address in Detroit. While I was in Georgia, the check came, and my mom in Detroit took my two hundred and fifty dollar check, cashed it, and spent it. I didn't get one penny of it and I didn't have any more money to boot. I was busted, disgusted, and couldn't be trusted.

At this point, with no money, no job, and

not having passed my welding test, I was feeling pretty low and became depressed. I knew I could not go back and live with my mom and Lucky in Detroit and I felt like a burden on my dad and my second mom. It was a bad time for me and I felt almost like killing myself, until one day while I was walking in downtown Atlanta, I saw a huge sign on a door that read "U.S. Army." The guy on the picture looked happy enough so I said to myself, "let me go in and check this out." I met with a recruiter and he told me all the great things about being in the Army and I felt I had another chance at life. I took the test and passed it and from that moment I was headed to the Army. About two weeks later, my recruiter picked me up from my dad and second mom's house in Scottdale, GA. It was raining that day, daddy and mom both hugged me then they said "goodbye." I was put on a bus with some other recruits and sent to Fort Jackson SC. When I arrived at Fort Jackson, we were sent to the reception center and welcomed. It seemed like it would be a picnic. I said, "this is going to be a breeze." After a week we were put on another bus, and sent to what they called, drag ass hill for basic training. The drill sergeants started cursing and yelling at us, *"Get off the fucking bus, move your asses, get down and push up Fort Jackson."* Several of the other guys immediately hit the ground and started doing push-ups but I'm like, who in the hell do they think they are talking too. I'm from Detroit, and straight out of Job Corps, they need to recognize and show me some respect. I angrily went towards the guy doing the yelling and my platoon sergeant stood up and got in front of me and the guy. My sergeant turned to him first and said *"Don't be messing with my men"* and then he turned around to me and said *"If something doesn't pertain to you, let it go in one ear and out the other."* I calmed down and from that moment on I followed his advice for a good while, and made it through basic training. When I made it to A.I.T. (Adult Individual Training), it was like going back to school. I started out as a clerk typist, and couldn't type worth a damn. They noticed my difficulty with typing and switched me to auto mechanics. I was only fair with that and if it wasn't for one of my best army buddies, who I consider a real brother "Mo" (God rest his soul) I wouldn't have made it through school. Mo could fix almost anything on a vehicle and man he really helped me.

Mo, another one of our partners from his home town, and I used to smoke some serious Columbo as he called it, get our drink on, and party like a mother for ya! Mo would talk that "splee" (as we called it) to me, he would say, *"Allen we are going to get us some "co – liz – biz", and we are going to get "fizzed – dizzed"* (translation, get some Columbian weed, and get fucked up). Mo and I had to part ways after school. I went to Ft. Carson, Colorado, and Mo went to Germany.

After I was transferred to my permanent duty station at Ft. Carson, Colorado I met this one girl at a gas station and she was fine as hell! I wanted to get in them draws from the start, but instead we ended up being like brother and sister. I met her whole family and they

became like my family. She lived with her mom
I could go over to their house, listen to music,
eat, or whatever I felt like doing. I still call her
mother my mom to this day and I will always
love them with my whole heart! I may not have
been "knocking her boots", but that uniform I
was wearing was paying off with a bunch of
other babes.

One other person I first met at Fort
Carson was my partner Jackson. Everyone
called him Jackson but I called him Jack. Jack
and I hung out at the NCO club, and at the
bowling alley on base. The NCO club back in
1976 was always jumping, and packed with
people. Jackson taught me how to bowl and I
am not lying, this skinny fellow bowled a three
hundred on several of occasions. His method

was to clutch the ball with both hands, take a few steps, cross his legs, and throw the ball with a curve where the ball would always come to the center and bam "a strike." He was the bomb. One night while at the bowling alley Jack and I ran into these two cute babes Denise, and Paula. I started dating Denise, and Jack began dating Paula. Neither one of these relationships worked out. I was wild and reckless at the time and it was the same old song; when it came to any relationship I was in, I always thought I was in love. Denise was letting me come over to her mother's house, listen to music, and do it with her on the kitchen floor while her mother was in the other room. Denise was the first one to mention orgy to me. When she told me that an orgy was a bunch of people getting together and doing it I said *"Hell no!"* If I was wild she was super wild. I felt I loved her and we were a couple, but to my surprise and dismay, I found out Denise was messing with this older man behind my back. Apparently he was a truck driver and she was doing it with this dude in the back of his rig which was parked outside Paula's house. Jack told me he saw them together. I really didn't know what to do. I wanted to kick both of their asses. The next thing I knew I went over to Denise's house. I was very angry and when she came to the door, I slapped the shit out of her without asking any questions or before she could say a word, which I totally regretted afterwards. Her mother was home at the time, and she yelled out to her mother *"This mother fucker hit me!"* and before anyone could get further charged up, I simply left. We never spoke again after that. I was hurt and angry when it happened but once I calmed down I thought about apologizing and maybe trying to get back with her, but I knew I had crossed the line. I knew there was no chance for us after what had happened. I have found that violence is never good or hitting a lady is simply something a man should never do. I felt really bad after this. This action cost me dearly because I felt that I would never get the chance to develop a real relationship. I have learned that I don't have a right to put my hands on anybody, and they don't have a right to put their hands on me.

Around this same time, tragedy struck my life really hard. I was notified that my sister Gail was in the hospital with a brain hemorrhage and I needed to come quickly to Detroit. I got leave

from the army and went straight home. When I
got to the hospital my sister was lying on a bed
hooked up to a machine that was breathing for
her. I tried talking to her but received no
response. I prayed to God that he would let her
live because she was such a sweet and beautiful
person and I loved my sister very much. We had
so many great memories together. But it wasn't
meant to be. The doctor's met with the family
and the decision was made to take her off the
life support machine because she was too far
gone and the doctor's had done all they could
do. My sister Gail died at twenty-one years old.
I was more than hurt. I went to the funeral and
somehow got through it but I was definitely not
over it.

In the military, as with civilian life, along

with good people come the bad. Right after I came back to Ft. Carson, Colorado after my sister Gail's funeral, this white Captain slapped me in my face four times. He said to me *"You are always having problems with this, or that, your sister's death and everything else."* I felt it was because he simply didn't like me for whatever reason, and felt he could get away with it. It was only by the grace of God that I didn't open fire on him! I was totally pissed but held my peace. I later reported it to my superiors. They took down my complaint but didn't seem too ready to do anything about it. I didn't hear anything from anyone, so after a couple of weeks, I asked a few other officers and high-ranking military personnel, *"What did you all do to the Captain?"* The reply was *"We took the appropriate action."* After this incident I decided that I couldn't take it any more so I went A.W.O.L. (absent without leave.) I hit the road walking, trying to hitch hike back to Detroit. I made it as far as Nebraska, ran out of money and ended up in jail when some cops stopped me and I didn't have any ID. I refused to give them my name so they took me to some crazy house. I finally told the people there that I was in the military. The next thing I knew they had me on my way back to Ft. Carson. I was taken to the military hospital. I know the captain and his crew were glad that I went A.W.O.L because I was then placed in a military hospital away from them. I stayed there for a while and then they gave me a medical discharge under honorable conditions after diagnosing me with paranoid schizophrenia. I didn't agree with that diagnosis because it seemed that some people would label you with what they wanted you to have and it wouldn't necessarily be the problem at all. I refused to buy into that label, not even for a disability check, but nevertheless, I was given a disability rating with an honorable discharge and a plane ticket to Detroit on the first thing smoking. I didn't get the chance to say goodbye to my friend Jack or anyone else.

Once back in Detroit, I headed straight for my old neighborhood to find my friends, but most were gone or were moving on with their lives, working, and raising kids. Everyone had grown up in the mist of my leaving Detroit, going to Job Corps at the age of sixteen, living for a while with my dad in Georgia, and then joining the Army. Wow! What a difference just a few years can make. The house parties were a thing of the past. I moved in with my brother Craig and my mom. My mom was raising my sister Gail's two children and believe it or not, Lucky was still in the picture but they were no longer living together. Somehow he and my mom split but she would see him occasionally. I couldn't help but think that after all we went through as children with the drinking and fighting between the both of them, not to mention him bullying me, and throwing me to the floor to the point where I vowed to kill him, she waited until we left home, before she moved out on her own for good. I couldn't understand it then and even now I don't understand why.

It was a bit of a struggle for me dealing with what I went through in the army and now finding myself back in the old neighborhood of

Detroit which was no longer as familiar to me. I did run into some old friends, and I met some new ones on Lemay Street. Lemay Street is where my mom relocated to after leaving Lucky for good. I consider most of the people on Lemay to be my family also. To let off some steam I joined the local Karate studio which helped me improve my fighting skills but also I learned to relax more. In addition to that, I figured I needed to do something more with my time so I got a job with a security company that hired me on the spot and I started attending community college. While I was being a player and dealing with nine women at the time, I also met and would eventually marry a girl I met at a grocery store. I made her my main lady but I wasn't exactly convinced on the marriage thing yet. I still had problems getting readjusted to civilian life and dealing with the memory of the captain

slapping me but I kept pushing forward. After a

couple of months back in Detroit I received a

letter from the VA that I had to meet with a

doctor in Chicago. I went to see him and he

gave me some sort of psychological

evaluation. He asked me what I had been doing

since leaving the Army, if I had a job, or was

attending school. I told him all about my job,

school, and my girlfriend. We talked for a while

and then I headed back home to Detroit. Within

less than a month my disability was

discontinued and I was no longer receiving any

assistance from the military. I received a notice

from them that the report from the doctor I had

spoken to in Chicago had determined I was not

paranoid schizophrenic. Because my life was

taking so many new turns at the time I decided

to focus on more positive things and not pursue questioning why I was diagnosed that way in the first place. I've had three doctors since then to tell me "there is nothing wrong with you." I searched for the right answers, and found them.

When I got back to Detroit I was at the height of doing my player thing, but actually fell in love and ended up marrying the young lady that I met at the grocery store. She poured so much love on me that I put on the brakes for her, and bam! I married her. She had joined the Air Force and after we tied the knot she left Detroit and I joined up with her later. We spent twelve years together, and had two fantastic boys. We tried to deal with all the ups and downs and turn-a- rounds that often come along in many relationships but it was a losing battle. Neither one of us was perfect in how we treated each other, so after a while, it just became too much and we split for good. After that I decided to move on from the past. Although I loved Detroit and still do in my heart and soul, I never returned to Detroit to stay. One of my sisters suggested that I move to Atlanta because she felt there was too much trouble in Detroit. I believe she was referring to when my brother Craig was tragically killed in a fight at the age of twenty one. Some guy ran over him with a car. She said "I'm afraid that you'll get killed." I will never be afraid of Detroit. I still have my Detroit swagger, and I am a boss, I'm a boss for Jesus. My family and friends will always have my back, and I will always have theirs. Shout outs to my whole lower Eastside family of Detroit! I moved back to Georgia, received my Master Barber's license from Brown's Barber College and remarried a very, very lovely and special lady (a true Godsend).

Although I've always been aware of God, turning my life over fully to the Lord has been a work in progress. In the beginning I had so many questions and challenged everything anyone was trying to teach me. I was familiar with my life as it was and although it was not ideal it was my place of upbringing. I was rooted in the life style I was introduced to as a child and that I lived much of my adult life. I will always love Detroit the place where I was born and raised. Someday I may move back if that's where God directs my life. I continue to grow and learn each day on my journey. I am not a perfect person by any means but I strive to be the person God would have me to be. My faith in God, his son Jesus, and the Holy Spirit are

my strengths.

EPILOGUE

From the Black Bottom in Detroit to this day my life has been one incredible journey filled with twists, turns, ups and downs. Every life change and lesson learned led me to my transformation – my revelation and acceptance of Jesus Christ (Yeshua).

Thank you Jesus, I am on my way! I feel liberated (free) with God my father, the Holy Spirit, and Jesus my savior.

"DETROIT, I WILL ALWAYS LOVE AND COME BACK TO YOU."

Omari Khalfani

(DETROIT YOU JUST HAVE TO LOVE IT!)

CONTACT

To contact the author or order additional copies please email <u>Redeemed5103@yahoo.com.</u> Send your name, address, telephone number, and number of desired copies or Mail your request to Author, P.O. box 673, Stockbridge, GA 30281. Please allow up to 3 weeks for delivery. Multiple book discount available.

www.ingramcontent.com/pod-product-compliance
Lightning Source LLC
Chambersburg PA
CBHW051253170626
46809CB00004B/1632